nesha GOES GREEN

words by Lakshmi Thamizhmani

art by Debasmita Dasgupta

Barefoot Books

Step inside a story

Prema breathed in deep, inhaling the sweet smells of incense and jasmine in the air. The market bustled with crowds shopping for Ganesha statues, paper umbrellas and mango-leaf decorations for the upcoming Ganesha Chaturthi* festival.

*guh-NAY-shah chuh-THUR-thee

Everyone came together to celebrate Ganesha,
the elephant-headed Hindu god of new beginnings.
They fasted, chanted prayers and offered coconut-
jaggery dumplings. At the end of the festival,
they placed Ganesha statues in the river.

But every year, the painted plaster statues fell apart, choking the city's river, harming its fish and polluting the water that fed the crops and people. The chemicals in the paints had made Prema's mother sick and unable to work or afford living in the city, forcing them to move to the village.

On her way to fetch water, Prema stopped by a statue shop and asked, "Do your statues harm the river?"

"My statues are beautiful, not harmful!" The statue seller scowled. "Newspapers print nonsense!"

Shaking her head, Prema walked away.

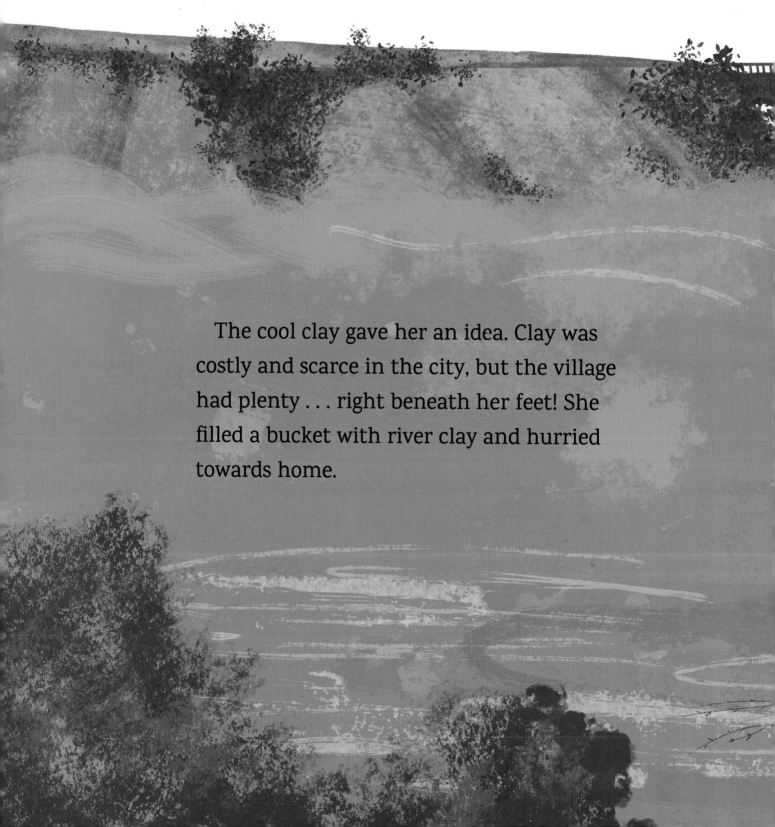

Meandering through the market, she reached
the riverbank. The river shone like a sea of sparkly
jewels. Prema stepped into it. Her bare feet sank
into the smooth, silky earth.

The cool clay gave her an idea. Clay was
costly and scarce in the city, but the village
had plenty . . . right beneath her feet! She
filled a bucket with river clay and hurried
towards home.

On her way back, she ran into her friends.

"We're going to the temple to get payasam prasadam*. Want to join us?" her best friend, Mani, asked.

Every day, the priest offered sweet payasam prasadam to Ganesha in worship and distributed them to devotees after prayer. Prema's tongue tingled at the tempting thought of the warm, sugary pudding melting in her mouth.

*PAA-yuh-suhm pruh-SAA-duhm

"Maybe later," Prema replied, feeling the weight of the clay in her bucket. "I have to work on a very important project first."

Back home, Prema imagined how her Ganesha would look. She made two balls and set one on top of the other.

Plop! The slippery clay didn't hold its shape.

My Ganesha looks nothing like the others, she thought.

She tried again, this time drying the clay to harden it.
But her hands couldn't create what her mind had pictured.

Remembering that Ganesha was the lord of removing
obstacles, she said a quiet prayer.

Prema studied a painting of Ganesha, then rolled two spheres, one for Ganesha's head and the other for his body. She shaped logs for his trunk, hands and legs. Then she added flaps for his ears and a crown for his head. Finally, Prema sat back and smiled at her work.

"Amma, see what I made."
Prema showed the statue to her mother.

"It's natural and unique. If only everyone
had one," Amma sighed.

Encouraged, Prema collected and prepared more clay.
She sculpted another Ganesha. And another, and another.
But there were too many Ganeshas to make and
only one Prema.

"Are you making statues for the entire village?" the statue seller taunted. "Clay statues can crack. Nobody will want them for prayers."

People flooded the statue seller's shop to buy plaster statues. Prema's eyes swelled with tears.

I can patch my clay statues if they crack, but my few statues won't be enough to keep the river clean, she thought. *If only I had four hands like Ganesha, I could make more statues faster.*

DONNNNNNNG!
DONNNNNNNNG!

Temple bells gonged in melodic rhythms.

Prema dashed to meet Mani.

"You made this? All by yourself?" Mani asked. "I haven't seen any like it at the market."

"It's small and will dissolve without poisoning the water. I can't let another river become polluted and make people like my amma sick," Prema said. "But I can't make a difference by myself."

Mani smiled. "Maybe not . . . but together, we can. Will you help me make a statue?"

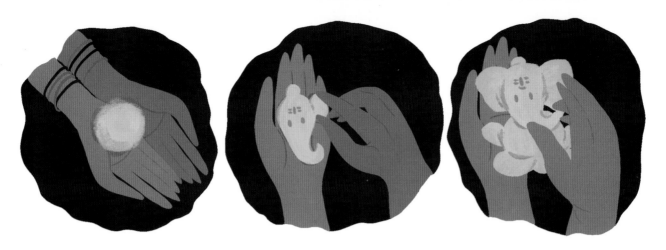

Their friends Raavi, Kumari, Amir,
Noor and Deepa crowded around.
"That looks like fun!" they chorused.

"And they're natural and safe for the river,"
Prema and Mani replied.

"Can you teach us?"

"Sure!"

As Prema and
Mani collected more
clay and water, Raavi set
up a makeshift statue-making
stand using old wooden boxes. Kumari and Noor gathered seeds
for the statues' eyes. For decoration, Deepa and Amir made leaf
umbrellas and garlands from cactus flowers and Bermuda grass.

Prema chanted, "Ganesha goes green. Let's keep our river clean!"

More kids flocked to learn from Prema and her friends. The children got busy teaching each other and making more statues, painting them with natural dyes and decorating them with flowers, grass and leaves.

Over the next few days, the village celebrated Ganesha Chaturthi.

At the end of the festival, dancing to drumbeats, Prema joined a singing sea of people taking their statues to the river.

Most people brought plaster statues but Mani, Raavi, Amir,
Kumari, Deepa, Noor and all their friends carried clay ones.
"Ganesha goes green. Let's keep the river clean!" they cheered.

"Your statues are the talk of the village," Mani's dad said.

"I must admit, your statues are a hit!" the statue seller said.
"Can we team up next year to make more?"

Prema's heart overflowed with happiness. The river glistened like a golden ribbon in the sunlight.

As Prema stepped into the river, the cool clay tickled her bare feet. She placed her Ganesha in the water.

People chanted, "Come again soon, Ganesha!"

Prema whispered to the river, "We'll take care of you." She watched her statue become one with the water and the earth.

ABOUT GANESHA CHATURTHI

Ganesha (*guh-NAY-shuh*) is worshipped in India and in other parts of the world as the four-handed, elephant-headed Hindu god of new beginnings and the remover of obstacles. Celebrated during the sixth month of the Hindu calendar (August or September in the solar calendar), the Ganesha Chaturthi (*guh-NAY-shah chuh-THUR-thee*) festival brings together people from different social backgrounds. According to some stories, the festival marks Ganesha's birthday, while others say it is to celebrate his arrival on earth to bless his followers.

All over India, huge Ganesha statues are installed on temporary stages for public worship. Smaller statues are bought and decorated with grass, flowers and umbrellas at home. People worship Ganesha by offering his beloved dumplings made of coconut and jaggery (a type of sugar), which he is always shown holding in his hand. The festival is celebrated for ten days. On the tenth day, people carry the statues in a parade and place them in flowing water, such as a river or sea, to represent the circle of life.

Some states in India have banned Ganesha statues made of painted plaster because they pollute the river or ocean water when they dissolve, which hurts the fish and animals that live in that water. To protect the environment, some people place their statues in water tubs built specially for the festival. Others choose to celebrate with eco-friendly statues made from clay, seeds and other natural materials, like Prema and her friends.

MAKE YOUR OWN EARTH-FRIENDLY STATUE!

HOMEMADE SCULPTING DOUGH

Adult helper needed

You'll need:

- 1 cup (150 g) all-purpose / plain flour
- ½ teaspoon salt
- 1 cup (240 mL) water
- 1 tablespoon cooking oil

Instructions:

1. In a saucepan, stir all the ingredients over medium heat for around 10 minutes until the dough stops sticking to the sides of the pan. Keep the heat on medium so the dough doesn't burn.

2. Let the hot dough rest until cool.

3. Knead the dough. If the dough is still a bit sticky, mix in some dry flour. Your sculpting dough is ready!

SCULPTING A STATUE

Instructions:

1. Decide what kind of statue to make. You could make an animal you love, a person you know, a character from a story or something else.

2. Roll balls and logs of your sculpting dough to make the shapes for your statue's body parts.

3. Stick them together or use toothpicks to hold them together.

4. Use seeds, flowers and other decorations to finish the details on your statue.

Earth-friendly decoration ideas:

- pebbles
- seeds
- rice grains
- leaves
- flowers
- toothpicks (to help hold pieces together)

For all the children trying to make a difference in the world — L. T.

To my mentor, Martin Ursell — D. D.

AutHOR'S NOte

As much as I love Ganesha Chaturthi, my heart ached when I learned that the beautiful statues caused water pollution. I decided to find eco-friendly ways to celebrate, and found that clay statues are a safe alternative. But they are not as popular as plaster statues! This concept evolved into Prema's story in *Ganesha Goes Green*. What could you do differently to inspire change like Prema?

— Lakshmi Thamizhmani

iLLUstRAtOR'S NOte

Growing up in India, festivals always meant something larger than your immediate family. It meant diverse communities coming together and celebrating with the same spirit. When I was illustrating Prema's story, I relived those childhood memories — the patterns, textures and emotions in people and the places where they happily coexist. I used local fabric motifs and kolam art design from Tamil Nadu, where Prema lives, to create the mixed-media illustrations for this book.

— Debasmita Dasgupta

Barefoot Books would like to thank Anne Cohen, Emily Golightly, Amala Reddie and Dr. Melody Ann Ross for their expert input in the creation of this book.

Barefoot Books
23 Bradford Street, 2nd Floor
Concord, MA 01742

Barefoot Books
29/30 Fitzroy Square
London, W1T 6LQ

Photo credits p.30 (top to bottom): © Aayushi Agarwal, Snehal Jeevan Pailkar/ Shutterstock.com, Vinayak Jagtap / Shutterstock.com
Reproduction by Bright Arts, Hong Kong. Printed in China
This book was typeset in Karma, Kaushan Script and Kindness Matters
The illustrations were prepared using digital techniques

Text copyright © 2023 by Lakshmi Thamizhmani
Illustrations copyright © 2023 by Debasmita Dasgupta
The moral rights of Lakshmi Thamizhmani and Debasmita Dasgupta have been asserted

Hardback ISBN 978-1-64686-997-8
Paperback ISBN 978-1-64686-998-5
E-book ISBN 979-8-88859-027-0

First published in the United States of America by Barefoot Books, Inc and in Great Britain by Barefoot Books, Ltd in 2023
All rights reserved

British Cataloguing-in-Publication Data: a catalogue record for this book is available from the British Library

Library of Congress Cataloging-in-Publication Data is available under LCCN 2023931023

Graphic design by Lindsey Leigh, Barefoot Books
Edited and art directed by Lisa Rosinsky, Barefoot Books
Editorial assistance by Aayushi Agarwal, Barefoot Books

135798642

Barefoot Books
step inside a story

At Barefoot Books, we celebrate art and story that opens the hearts
and minds of children from all walks of life, focusing on themes that
encourage independence of spirit, enthusiasm for learning and respect
for the world's diversity. The welfare of our children is dependent on
the welfare of the planet, so we source paper from sustainably managed
forests and constantly strive to reduce our environmental impact.
Playful, beautiful and created to last a lifetime, our products combine
the best of the present with the best of the past to educate our
children as the caretakers of tomorrow.

www.barefootbooks.com

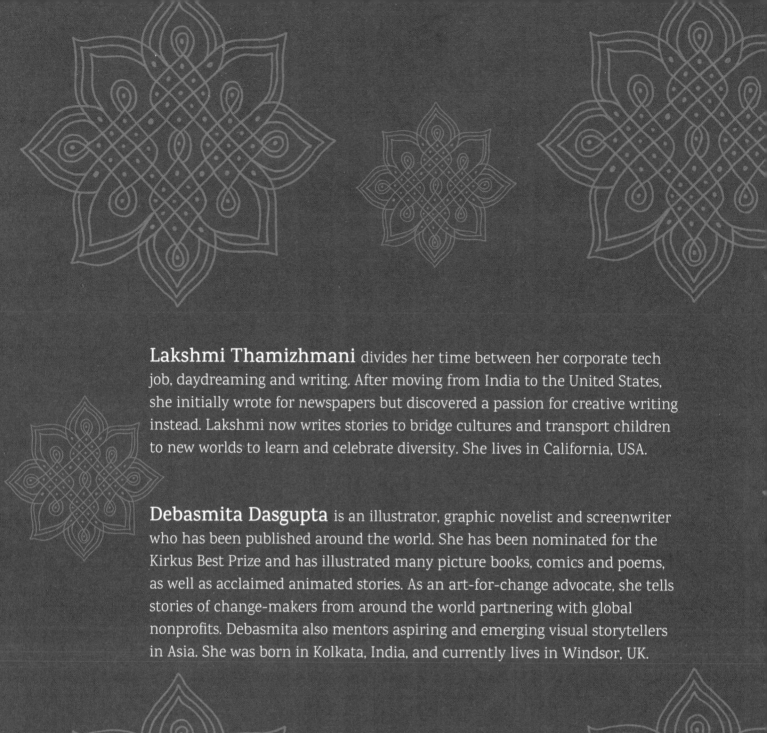

Lakshmi Thamizhmani divides her time between her corporate tech job, daydreaming and writing. After moving from India to the United States, she initially wrote for newspapers but discovered a passion for creative writing instead. Lakshmi now writes stories to bridge cultures and transport children to new worlds to learn and celebrate diversity. She lives in California, USA.

Debasmita Dasgupta is an illustrator, graphic novelist and screenwriter who has been published around the world. She has been nominated for the Kirkus Best Prize and has illustrated many picture books, comics and poems, as well as acclaimed animated stories. As an art-for-change advocate, she tells stories of change-makers from around the world partnering with global nonprofits. Debasmita also mentors aspiring and emerging visual storytellers in Asia. She was born in Kolkata, India, and currently lives in Windsor, UK.

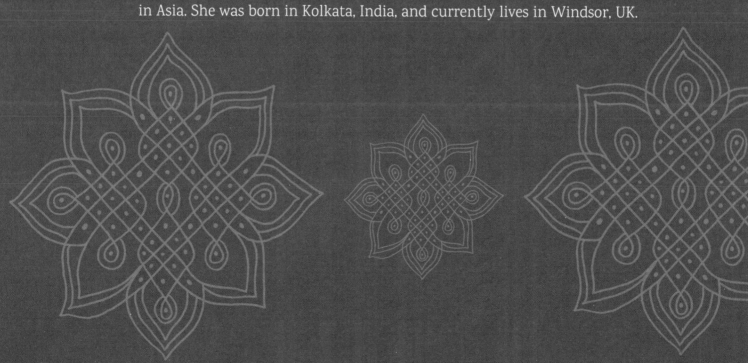